# Cooper Clark
## and the Dragon Lady

by Valerie Sherrard
illustrations by David Jardine

Fitzhenry & Whiteside

Published in Canada by Fitzhenry & Whiteside,
195 Allstate Parkway, Markham, ON   L3R 4T8

Published in the United States by Fitzhenry & Whiteside,
311 Washington Street, Brighton, MA  02135

**Library and Archives Canada Cataloguing in Publication**
Title: Cooper Clark and the dragon lady / Valerie Sherrard.
Names: Sherrard, Valerie, author.
Identifiers: Canadiana 20190167866 | ISBN 9781554554621 (softcover)
Classification: LCC PS8587.H3867 C66 2019 | DDC jC813/.6—dc23

**Publisher Cataloging-in-Publication Data (U.S.)**
Names: Sherrard, Valerie, author.
Title: Cooper Clark and the Dragon Lady / Valerie Sherrard.
Description: Markham, Ontario : Fitzhenry & Whiteside, 2019. | Summary: "This delightful
chapter book introduces young readers to Cooper Clark, whose world takes an alarming turn
when his regular babysitter gets a new job. Arrangements are then made for Cooper to spend
his after school hours with old Mrs. Mulligan, a plan he does not care for one bit! Everyone
knows that Mrs. Mulligan has a real live dragon in her basement and although he has kept
his fears secret, Cooper is very afraid of dragons. In order to avoid Mrs. Mulligan's dreadful
pet, Cooper comes up with one zany plan after another" -- Provided by publisher.
Identifiers: ISBN 978-1-55455-462-1 (paperback)

Subjects: LCSH: Dragons -- Juvenile fiction. | Fear -- Juvenile fiction. | Babysitters --
Juvenile fiction. | BISAC: JUVENILE FICTION / General. | JUVENILE FICTION / Social
Themes / Friendship.
Classification: LCC PZ7.S547Coo |DDC [F] – dc23

10 9 8 7 6 5 4 3 2 1

Fitzhenry & Whiteside acknowledges with thanks the Canada Council for the Arts
for their support of our publishing program. We acknowledge the financial support of the
Government of Canada through the Canada Book Fund (CBF) for our publishing activities.

Canada Council   Conseil des arts
for the Arts     du Canada

Text and cover design by Tanya Montini
Printed in Canada by Houghton Boston

www.fitzhenry.ca

For Matthew and Andrew,

2/3<sup>rds</sup> of the Happy Love Band

Some people like dragons. My friends Jared and Nina like them a lot. They have books and movies about dragons. Nina even has a stuffed dragon that sits on a tiny rocking chair in her bedroom. She calls it Kiwi because it is bright green. She tries to get me to hug it.

She holds it out to me and says, "Look, Cooper! Kiwi loves you."

When she does that I cross my arms and shake my head.

"It's your dragon, *you* hug it," I tell her.

"Cooper! You are hurting Kiwi's feelings," Nina says. She puts out her bottom lip and makes sad eyes at me.

I do not care. Because I do *not* like dragons.

I don't like dragon books or movies or toys. There is a dragon in one of our toy bins at school. If you squeeze its tail the eyes flash and it makes a crackly, roaring sound. Sometimes other kids in my class argue about who gets to play with it and our teacher Mr. Ritter has to hold up his hand.

"No squabbling, children," he says. "Remember to share and use your best manners or I will have to send somebody to the quiet chair."

I never have to worry about going to the quiet chair over the dragon.

Up until today, everything was fine. I stayed away from dragons and they stayed away from me. But then—disaster!

Because today, two terrible things happened.

The first terrible thing happened at my babysitter's house. I go there every day after school until my mother or father comes to pick me up. My mother and father both have jobs. That is why they are not home when I get out of school and that is why I go to a babysitter.

I love my babysitter! Her name is Linda and she is the best babysitter in the

whole entire world. Linda plays games with me and she is always a good sport if she loses, which happens a lot.

"Not again!" she says when I win. She puts the back of her hand on her forehead and makes a sad face.

But then she laughs because she doesn't really mind. And she hugs me and says, "How about a snack to celebrate your great victory, Cooper?"

Most of the time Linda gets me a snack that is approved. That means it is something my mom and dad say is all right for me to eat before supper. Approved snacks are things like fruit or yogurt.

But every now and then Linda whispers, "Maybe today we will have a snack that is not approved. What do you think?"

"That is a great idea," I whisper back, even though there is no one else there to hear us.

Then Linda gets me a cookie or cupcake or ice cream or some other delicious treat that is not approved.

The first time that happened I thought it would be a secret. After I finished my snack I wiped my mouth and checked my shirt to make sure there were no tell-tale crumbs.

But when my dad came to the door, Linda told him all about it.

"I'm afraid I have something bad to report," she said. "I made jam-filled cookies this morning and I could not stop myself from giving one to Cooper."

"I see," said my father.

"I'm very sorry," Linda said.

"I think we can let it go this time," my dad said.

Linda always tells on herself when she gives me a snack that is not approved. And today was one of those days. Today she gave me a lemon tart with whipped cream on it. I knew she would confess when it was time for me to get picked up.

Sure enough, when Mom came to the door, Linda said, "I'm afraid I have something to tell you."

But it was not about the tart.

It was much, much worse.

"I have been offered a job at Monkey Bowl," Linda told my mother.

"MONKEY BOWL!" I yelled. "I LOVE that place, don't I, Mom?"

The yell made Mom jump a little but I couldn't keep it in. Monkey Bowl is my favourite place to go when we are getting a family treat. They make scrumptious ice cream and frozen yogurt desserts.

You choose your own toppings which is difficult because there are about a gazillion of them.

"I have decided to take the job," Linda said.

I could hardly believe that my very own babysitter was going to be working somewhere as delicious as Monkey Bowl.

My mom did not seem excited about it. All she said was, "I'm sure you will enjoy working there. When do you start?"

"Tomorrow," Linda said. Then she told us the bad thing.

"I'm afraid with this new job I will not be able to watch Cooper after school anymore."

My heart sank right into my shoes. My babysitter was quitting on me.

"But I love coming here!" I said.

"And I love having you," Linda said. "You're a great kid."

I wanted to ask Linda why she was taking a job that would not let her keep on babysitting me after school if she really loved having me. But my throat felt funny and that was making it hard to talk.

"I'm sorry about the short notice but the opportunity came up suddenly," Linda told Mom.

"I understand," Mom said.

Then Linda said her sister Manda could help out until Mom found a new sitter. That did not sound good to me. Manda took care of me one time when Linda had to go to the dentist. She was not fun like Linda. Manda did not play games or read with me. She wanted me to play quietly by myself, which is not easy. And when I was having my snack, she told me four times to sit up straight.

"I don't think I will need Manda," Mom said. "There are a few sitters I can check with first. Tell your sister thank you for the offer anyway.

Linda squatted down and hugged me. She said, "You can come and visit me anytime, Cooper."

"Okay," I said. I felt sad but also happy because Linda wanted me to visit her even though she would not be babysitting me anymore.

At supper time Mom told Dad that Linda had gotten a different job and I would need a new sitter.

"That's too bad," Dad said. "Linda was excellent."

"We can go to see her at her job at Monkey Bowl anytime we want," I said helpfully.

"Monkey Bowl?" said Dad. "Count me in!" He held up his hand for a high five. I smacked my hand on his and we both smiled.

Mom rolled her eyes and said, "You guys and your junk food!"

Mom is very serious about eating healthy. We do that most of the time but not when we go to Monkey Bowl. When we go there Mom always says she is only going to get a small treat but then she orders a medium.

"Where is Cooper going to go after

school from now on?" Dad asked.

"I will make a few calls when supper is over," Mom said. "I'm sure I will find someone."

After we finished eating and tidying up the kitchen, Mom called someone named Jess and someone else named Maureen. I was in one of my secret listening places when she told Dad about those calls. That is how I knew Jess had moved away and Maureen was taking care of the Allman twins. After that Mom called two more people.

I heard her tell Dad, "No luck. I might have to get Linda's sister Manda after all."

"Manda is CRABBY," I said.

Mom stuck her head around the corner, leaned down, and saw me.

"Are you spying on me, Cooper?" Mom asked.

"No," I said. "I am only listening."

"You know you are not supposed to say rude things about people," Mom said. But after that she did not say anything else about getting Manda to babysit.

"I have an idea," Dad said. "What about Mrs. Mulligan?"

My heart started to tremble. My mouth got very dry.

Mrs. Mulligan lives at the end of our street, right on the corner. All the kids in the neighbourhood know things about her. Her glasses are so big they hide half of her face and she wears a sweater no matter how hot it is outside. I have heard that she feeds peculiar snacks like bread with applesauce on it to the children she babysits.

But that is not the worst thing.

The worst thing is—Mrs. Mulligan has a dragon in her basement!

I crossed my fingers. I closed my eyes and wished as hard as I could.

My wish was that Mrs. Mulligan would say NO when Mom called to ask her if she would babysit me after school.

But my wish did not work. Mrs. Mulligan said YES.

"She said she would be HAPPY to watch you," Mom told me. She was smiling like this was very good news.

That is because Mom doesn't know that there is a dragon in Mrs. Mulligan's basement. Also, Mom does not know that I do not like dragons.

But there is one other thing. It is not just that I don't LIKE dragons.

It is also that...

I am...very, very,

ever so,

extraordinarily

AFRAID of dragons.

That is a hard thing to tell. I have not even told that to my best friends Jared and Nina. Because what if they laugh and tease me?

The only person in the whole entire world I have *ever* told is my cat, Howard.

Howard is excellent at keeping secrets. Also, he does not care for dragons either so he understands exactly how I feel.

But my friends would not understand. They might say there are no dragons where we live. Besides that they will probably tell me that dragons are only pretend.

That is what most people think but I am not so sure.

I have heard things about Mrs. Mulligan's dragon from Lenny and Matt. They are two older kids on our street who used to go to Mrs. Mulligan's after school.

They told me Scout's Honour that the dragon in Mrs. Mulligan's basement is real.

Matt said that the dragon is not always in its special dragon house. He said that sometimes it runs all over the basement.

And Lenny said the dragon has a pointy pink tongue. The dragon smiles and sticks his tongue out and that is how you know he is about to pounce.

Why would I want to go somewhere that a dragon might pounce on me at any moment? Or even just smile and stick out a pointy pink tongue?

I had to talk Mom out of sending me to Mrs. Mulligan's house! Only, I knew if I told her it was because a dragon lived there she would think I was telling tall tales. So I started thinking. I thought and thought until I had an idea. It was a GREAT idea!

"I don't think I can go to Mrs. Mulligan's house after school," I said.

"Why not, Cooper?" Mom asked.

"Because—" I paused. I took a deep breath and made myself look very serious.

"Sometimes children go there and they are NEVER SEEN AGAIN!" I said. My mom and dad like me a lot. They would never take that kind of a chance.

"Is that so?" Mom said. She looked at Dad and they made strange faces at each other.

"Hokey doodle," Dad said. "That sounds serious."

"Maybe I should call some of these children's parents to find out what happened," Mom said.

"That's a great idea," Dad agreed.

"I don't think any of them have phones," I said.

"Talk about bad luck," said Dad.

I peeked over at Mom. Her eyebrows were up way higher than they normally are. That meant she was suspicious I was telling her a tall tale even though I had not said anything about the dragon. My mom is the suspicious type.

"What's the real reason you don't want to go to Mrs. Mulligan's house after school, Cooper?" she asked.

I could see that telling fibs wasn't going to work. Not even if it was an interesting fib. I needed to think of some other way to change Mom's mind, and quick.

"She's too old," I said.

"Too old for what?" Dad said.

"For taking care of a kid," I said.

"I see," Dad said. "So you're worried she won't be able to do some of the things a babysitter needs to do."

"Exactly," I agreed.

"What kinds of things—exactly?" Dad asked.

I thought about that for a minute. Then I said, "Sometimes old people can't see or hear too good."

"Anything else?" Dad asked.

"I guess not."

Mom smiled. "Well then, in that case I have good news for you."

"Is the good news that you aren't going to make me go there?" I said.

"No. The good news is that when I first called, Mrs. Mulligan mentioned she'd just been working on a thousand piece jigsaw puzzle."

"Wow," said Dad. "She must see

perfectly with her glasses."

"That's right," Mom said. "And she heard me just fine when we were talking."

"Excellent!" said Dad. He stuck a thumb up in the air. "I guess that's the end of your worries, Cooper."

"I guess," I said.

I knew then that I was going to have to think of some other way out of going to Mrs. Mulligan's house.

Because no way was I hanging around somewhere a dragon might get me.

I still had not thought of a way to get out of being babysat by the dragon lady by breakfast the next morning. That was not good.

I ate my cereal as slowly as I could, hoping a brilliant idea would pop into my head.

Dad told me, "Shake a leg, Cooper." That's his way of telling me to hurry up.

He took a gulp of coffee and made a sour face, which meant he forgot the sugar. He does that a lot.

I finished eating and put my bowl in the sink. It seemed there was only one thing to do. I turned around and looked at my mom and dad.

"I don't feel so good," I said. It was kind of true.

Mom waved her hand for me to come over to her. She checked my forehead with the back of her hand.

"No fever," she said.

"Maybe the fever didn't get all the way up to my head yet," I said.

"Is your stomach sick?" Dad asked.

"A little bit."

"I *did* notice that he took a long time

to eat his cereal," Dad told Mom.

Mom stood up and went to the sink. She rinsed her cup and plate and also my bowl and put them in the dishwasher. She did not look very worried.

"Maybe you should call Grandma to come over," I said. "In case I'm too sick to go to school."

"Let's see if you can make it to the bathroom to brush your teeth first," Mom said.

I walked down the hall with my head hanging as low as it could go. I let out some moans and groans as I walked and I also dragged my feet as slowly as I could. It seemed like my own mother didn't even care how sick I was.

All she cared about was making me brush my teeth.

I stopped walking. It's easier for me to think when I'm standing still.

I thought about the last thing Mom said, which was, "Let's see if you can make it to the bathroom to brush your teeth first."

But what if I *couldn't* make it to the bathroom? What then?

Then I remembered something about my Dad's great-aunt Jasmina. She was famous for taking fainting spells. I never saw it happen but I heard that when she fainted she had to lie down and fan herself.

That sounded just like the thing I needed. A good fainting spell.

The only problem was, I didn't exactly know what made a person faint. I guessed it would start off with getting dizzy though, and I had some ideas about that.

I held my breath. I held it and held it and held it until I thought I would burst. But it didn't make me faint.

Then I spun myself around. Around and around and around and around. When I stopped I tried to take a step but I didn't go very far. I lurched one way and then the other way, bumped into the wall and fell down.

I decided that was probably about the same thing as fainting. So I laid on the hallway floor and closed my eyes and stayed very, very still. I knew any minute Mom or Dad would come along and find me.

When they saw that I had fainted they would know there was no way I could go to school. I would have to stay home and lie around and fan myself.

Howard found me first. He nudged my chin with his head. He smacked my nose with his paw. I almost laughed but I stopped myself by thinking about the dragon.

Finally I heard Mom coming down the hall. I knew it was Mom because of the way her shoes clickety-clicked on the floor. When she got to me she stopped.

"Oh for goodness' sakes," she said. Then she called for my dad.

"What is it?" he asked.

"Cooper has left a pile of clothes on the floor." She stepped over me.

"Do you think I should pick these clothes up?" Dad asked.

"No, just leave them where they are,"

Mom said. "He has to learn to clean up after himself."

Then they both started to walk away.

I sat up.

"Hey!" I said. "It's me!"

"Cooper!" said Mom.

"Well would you look at that!" said Dad. "What are you doing on the floor?"

"I'm having a fainting spell," I said. "I bet I got it from your great-aunt Jasmina."

Mom and Dad looked at each other.

"I see," said Dad.

"Dear me," said Mom.

"I don't think I can go to school," I said. "Not until I get over this fainting business."

"You'd better lie down," Dad said. "Do you think you can walk or should I carry you to bed?"

"You'd better carry me," I said. "I probably need to be fanned too. Like your great-aunt Jasmina."

Dad scooped me up and carried me to my room.

"The couch might be better," I said. "So I can watch TV when I'm not fainted."

"I'll check with your mom," he said.

"She's probably calling Grandma," I told him. "Maybe she can ask if Grandma can bring some cookies when she comes."

Mom poked her head into my room.

"I'm afraid Grandma won't be coming," she said. "Or did you forget she and Grandpa went on a cruise with some of their friends?"

I had completely forgotten that.

"I'll just have to call Mrs. Mulligan to see if she can watch you for the whole day."

"No!" I yelled.

"Well, you can't go to school and be fainting all over the place," Mom said.

I jumped up. "I think I'm starting to feel better!"

Mom shook her head. "I don't know," she said.

"Really – I'm okay now!" I raced out my bedroom door and all the way down the hall. Then I ran back to my room, in and around the bed and back down the hall to the bathroom door.

"I'm going to brush my teeth now!" I yelled. I closed the door, only not all the way. I left it open a little bit so I could hear what they were going to say.

"That's settled then," Dad said.

"Yep," said Mom.

Whew! I might still be going to the dragon lady's house but at least I wouldn't be there all day long. Having to hide from a dragon for a whole day was the scariest thing I could imagine.

I got dressed and checked my lunch bag to make sure my lunch was inside. It cheered me up when I saw pineapple juice in there. Pineapple is the best juice in the world. I wish I had it every day. Dad says I would get tired of it then and

that's why they get me different kinds. I don't know if that's true because I never got to have it every day to find out.

Mom drove me to school. She told me to pay attention in class and to behave for my teacher and have a great day. She says the same things every time it's her turn to drive me.

Jared and Nina were already in our classroom when I went inside. Nina ran over to me.

"Hi, Cooper," she said. "Look at the AMAZING bracelet my sister Melanie made for me."

Nina has three older sisters. I can't remember which one is Melanie. Also, I did not care about the bracelet.

"Isn't it beautiful?" she asked.

She put her arm close to my face and shook it. It looked like a bunch of plastic strings tied together. I was not impressed.

"It's all different shades of purple!" she said.

"I can see what colour it is," I said.

"And don't you just love it?" she asked.

"It's okay I guess," I said.

"It's not just okay," she said. She shook it some more. "It's beautiful!"

I pushed her arm away. I said, "Stop waving it in front of my face."

Nina looked cross. "You aren't very nice," she said.

"Sorry," I said. "I'm in a grouchy mood today."

"How come?" Nina asked.

I just shrugged. There was no way I was

going to tell her what was bothering me.

Nina looked even crosser. She waved at Jared to come over. When he did she said, "Cooper is in a bad mood. Only he won't tell me why."

"I guess he doesn't have to if he doesn't want to," Jared told her. "Right, Cooper?"

"Right," I agreed.

Nina walked away stomping and mumbling. She started showing other kids her jangly purple bracelet.

"It looks like she's mad at you," Jared said.

"I don't care," I said. And mostly I didn't. Because I had other things to worry about.

Like dragons.

It was not a very good morning at school. For one thing, the teacher called on me to answer a question.

In our class you have to stand up if the teacher calls your name. I stood up but I didn't know the answer. That was because I didn't even know the question. Instead of paying attention I had been thinking about what I was going to do when I had to face that dragon at the end of the day.

I stood up. I looked at my shoes.

"Cooper?" said Mr. Ritter after a moment.

I didn't think it was a good idea to tell Mr. Ritter I had not been paying attention. So I just shook my head.

"I can't remember," I said.

"You can't remember what your middle name is?" Mr. Ritter asked. He sounded surprised.

Everyone laughed. A few kids pointed, which is not even allowed because pointing is rude. I was hoping Mr. Ritter would notice them and stop paying attention to me. That didn't happen.

"I think maybe somebody was day-dreaming," Mr. Ritter said. He meant me.

At lunchtime some of the kids came up to me and asked if I remembered my middle name yet. I pretended I didn't hear them. I pretended I was very, very busy looking to see what was in my lunchbox.

Then Terry Merkle came over. He stood there for a minute not saying anything. Finally, he lifted his hand. Terry was holding a baggy with two gray lumps in it.

"Want to trade anything for my cookies?" he asked. "They're really good."

Even if the cookies didn't look like lumps of modelling clay, I wouldn't have traded for them. Everyone in class knows Terry's mom makes the worst cookies in the whole entire world. At the start of the year she came to school and told us all about them.

"My son Terry will be bringing home-made cookies and other treats to school," she said. "I just want to let you know that if any of you have allergies, you do not need to worry." She explained that the things she bakes never contain nuts or dairy or a few other things that I never heard of before.

She forgot to mention that they also did not contain anything that tastes yummy. Back then, Terry tricked some of us into trading for those cookies once but no one ever made that mistake again. I bet not even a dragon would eat Terry Merkle's mother's baking.

That is why I told Terry, "No thanks."

It is also what gave me an idea. I picked up my lunch box and started walking around the class and before very long I had made three trades.

I traded my delicious pineapple juice for a pepperoni stick.

I traded my banana for a chunk of cheese.

I traded my blueberry granola bar for two chicken nuggets.

After that I ate my sandwich and got a drink of water from the fountain. It wasn't the greatest lunch ever. Trading away the best things in my lunch wasn't an easy thing to do but I had no choice. It was part of my new plan.

When nobody was looking, I stuffed the things I'd traded for into my pants pocket. It was important that they were somewhere I could grab them quick.

I was still trying to think of a way out of going to Mrs. Mulligan's house after school. But if I couldn't, I might need the pepperoni and the chunk of cheese and the chicken nuggets.

I might need them to give to the dragon. If the dragon was busy eating pepperoni and cheese and chicken nuggets, he might not think about eating me!

I could only hope the dragon wasn't very hungry!

Every day after school I take a bus. Jared and Nina take the same bus because Jared's house is near mine and his mom babysits Nina. My mom asked Jared's mom if I could go there too but Jared's mom said she already had her hands full.

Today we were the first ones on the bus so we got to sit in the long seat at the very back.

I sat right in the middle, which is the best spot.

That made Nina put on a mad face and cross her arms in front of her.

"It's my turn to sit in the middle!" she said. She always thinks it's her turn.

"Is not," I said. I didn't actually know whose turn it was but I wasn't in the mood to move for Nina. That girl is way too bossy.

Nina tried to push me to one side. I didn't budge.

"You're being a big meanie!" she yelled.

"Am not," I said.

She huffed and stomped her foot and turned around. Good, I thought to myself. Let her go sit somewhere else and sulk. That won't bother me.

Except that isn't what Nina did. She backed up and sat on top of me.

"Get off me!" I said. Her hair was hanging down, tickling my nose.

"No," she said. "It's my turn to sit in the middle and that's where I'm sitting."

I tried to push her off but she held on tight. So I wriggled side to side until I finally tipped her off.

"Ha!" I said. Then I realized I had accidentally squirmed myself to the side and tipped Nina off right into the middle of the seat. Right where she wanted to be!

She pushed her face in my direction and smiled with all her teeth.

"I'm in the middle!" she said, as if I couldn't already see that.

"Who cares?" I said.

"You're crabby!" Nina yelled. "Cooper's being a humungous grump, isn't he, Jared?"

"I'm not sure," said Jared. "Anyway, settle down before Mr. Finn makes us move to the front."

That warning put a stop to Nina's hollering. Everyone knows Mr. Finn does not tolerate bickering. He could come to the back seat any minute. Mr. Finn has some kind of super-power bus driver hearing. Every now and then he reminds us he hears everything that happens on his bus. He's the only person I know with a super power.

I wish I had a super power too—whatever kind you need to slay a dragon. Or at least keep it from sticking out its pointy pink tongue and pouncing.

Mostly, I wished my old sitter, Linda, never got a job at Monkey Bowl. Then I would still be going to her place after school.

That gave me a new idea. Maybe the best idea so far!

Because I suddenly remembered how Linda said I could visit her anytime! She said she would love to see me!

Well, Monkey Bowl is not that far. So I decided this would be an excellent day to go and visit Linda. It would be a wonderful surprise for her!

I bet Linda would be excited and delighted when I walked in.

She would probably give me a big hug and say, "Cooper! You came to visit me!"

And you know what else? She might say, "Sit right up here at the counter. I have a surprise for you too."

And then she'd get out the biggest bowl ever and make me the most amazing ice cream treat that's ever been made!

I was imagining what toppings Linda might put on my treat when I felt a sharp elbow jab into my side. It was Nina.

"What's the matter with you?" she asked.

"What do you mean?" I said.

"She means the weird face you're making," Jared said. He was leaning forward and staring at me.

"I'm not making a weird face," I said.

"Are so!" Nina giggled. "You're making a lovey-dovey, smushy-smiley face."

I decided I'd better stop thinking about what Linda might give me at Monkey Bowl.

Jared and Nina and I get off the bus at the same stop, in front of Jared's house. Mrs. Mulligan lives at the end of the block, right on the corner.

Monkey Bowl is in the same direction as Mrs. Mulligan's. That meant I would have to walk past her house, which could be tricky.

I was getting close when I noticed Mrs.

Mulligan standing out on her step. She was looking this way and that and I knew right away she was looking for me.

Uh, oh.

I ducked behind a bush and waited. Mrs. Mulligan kept looking. After a minute I heard her call out in a tiny, old person voice.

"Cooper! Cooper Clark? Where are you?"

It sounded exactly the same as when she calls her cat, Minette. I've heard her lots of times.

"Minette! Minette, my pet! Where are you?"

At least she didn't call me her pet.

I stayed still and waited. After a few minutes Mrs. Mulligan went back inside and closed the door. I crawled backward out of the bush and crept behind the house. I stayed out of sight of Mrs. Mulligan's place until I got far away enough that she couldn't see me.

I'd been so busy thinking about avoiding Mrs. Mulligan that I was a good block or two away from there before I noticed something strange.

There was a dog trotting along beside me. I knew his name was Rascal and I'd seen him around our block before but I'd never played with him or anything.

As I tried to figure out what Rascal was doing, another dog named Trixie raced up to join us. She also started running along beside me.

I stopped walking and looked back and

forth between them.

"What's up?" I said, even though I knew it was silly to ask dogs a question.

Rascal moved in closer. "Rowf!" he said.

"Yip! Yip!" said Trixie.

There was something about the way they kept getting closer and closer that was beginning to worry me.

Rascal nudged me with his nose and Trixie stood up on her back legs and leaned her pesky paws against my leg.

"Maybe you two should go home," I suggested. I was starting to get a nervous feeling in my stomach.

Rascal gave me another nudge but this time he used his whole head and I went sprawling on the ground.

They were on me in a flash! Rascal on

my left and Trixie on my right – snuffing and snorting and tugging at my pockets.

The next thing I knew, Trixie had a chicken nugget in her mouth and was racing away. Rascal wasn't in such a hurry. He found the pepperoni stick, gobbled it in one gulp, and went back for the cheese.

As I got back to my feet I reached into the other pocket and pulled out the second chicken nugget. It looked pretty small in my hand.

It was the only thing left from my lunch trades. I'd given up my pineapple juice and my banana and my blueberry granola bar for nothing. This little nugget wasn't going to keep a dragon from deciding I would make a nice juicy snack.

But then I remembered that was okay. I wasn't going to be seeing any nasty old dragon today. I was on my way to a tasty ice cream treat at Monkey Bowl.

"You might as well have this too," I said, holding out the last nugget. "I won't be needing it after all. And anyway, this isn't big enough to save me from a dragon."

Rascal swallowed it whole and made a happy dog sound. I'm pretty sure he was trying to tell me we were best friends now.

"Okay, well, I gotta go," I told him. I patted his head and started off again toward Monkey Bowl.

I could see Linda through the window. She was smiling and talking to a woman and two teenage boys. It looked like they were having a hard time deciding what to order. I didn't blame them. It's tough to pick when there are so many choices.

I got to the door and pushed it open. Once I was inside I stood in line behind the other customers. It was hard to stay quiet and wait until they finally made up their minds. After that, Linda had to make their treats, but at last they took their tray and went to sit at a table.

Then Linda saw me!

"Hi, Linda," I said.

"Cooper!" A huge smile burst onto her face and she clapped her hands. "What a nice surprise!"

I smiled right back at her. I hoped it wouldn't take too long before Linda got the idea to make me a treat. The sight of all the toppings was making my mouth water.

But all of a sudden Linda started looking behind me, and her smile wasn't so big anymore. She looked at the door for a minute and she looked all around the room. By that time, her smile was gone.

"Cooper?" she said. "Did you come here by yourself?"

"Yes! To surprise you!" I said.

Linda frowned. She said, "This is *not* good."

"I thought you would be happy to see me," I said.

"It's not about being happy to see you, Coop. It's about you coming here when you were supposed to go somewhere else."

I hung my head down. This was not going the way I thought it would.

Linda squatted in front of me. She put two fingers under my chin and very gently lifted my head up until I was looking at her.

"Someone is probably very worried about you right now," she said.

I did not say anything.

"Where were you supposed to go?" she asked.

"To Mrs. Mulligan's house," I said. "But I don't want to."

"Change can be hard, Cooper," Linda said quietly. "But it will be okay. You'll see."

I wanted to tell her about the dragon but I couldn't make myself say anything. I especially couldn't make myself say how scared I was of what it might do.

"You wait right here, Cooper," Linda said. She used the voice she uses when she wants me to know there is not going to be any nonsense from me.

She patted a stool and I got up on it while she went into a room at the back. I saw her talking on the telephone and I knew she was calling Mrs. Mulligan.

I wished those dogs had not eaten the pepperoni and cheese and chicken nuggets. Now I had no way to save myself if the dragon stuck out its pointy pink tongue and got ready to pounce on me.

I was doomed.

"Okay, Coop."

I looked up and saw that Linda was back. She put a dish with ice cream and chocolate cookie chunks in front of me.

"Mrs. Mulligan is on her way for you," she said. "You should have just enough time to eat this before she gets here."

"Thanks!" I picked up the spoon and dug in. It was super delicious. It was almost delicious enough to make me forget the danger I was about to face.

"I know you'll go where you're supposed

to from now on," Linda said when she took away the empty bowl. "And don't worry, kiddo. It will get easier."

I almost told her then. The words were right there—about the dragon and its tongue and even the part about being scared. Because I suddenly knew it would be all right to tell Linda. She wouldn't laugh or say I was being a big baby. And maybe she could have helped.

But I never found out.

Because at that very moment the door opened and there she stood.

Mrs. Mulligan.

The dragon lady.

My heart did a little jump. Then it sank.

"Goodness me!" said Mrs. Mulligan. "Cooper Clark, where have you been?"

That seemed like a silly question since she could see for herself.

"Sorry," I said.

"You've caused quite a stir, young man," Mrs. Mulligan said sternly. "I had to call your mother and you can just imagine how upset she was when I told her you were missing!"

Ulp. I hadn't thought about that. Now I was going to get into trouble when I got home.

"Why, when I called back to say you were here, the poor woman burst into tears of relief," Mrs. Mulligan added.

"There might have been a mix-up," Linda said. "I told Cooper to be sure to come and visit me sometime."

Then she told me she would call my mom to explain and smooth things over.

Linda is my hero.

"Into the car with you, then," Mrs. Mulligan said.

I got into the car. Mrs. Mulligan turned the key and after that it only seemed to take one single second of driving to reach her driveway. I swallowed hard. I knew I had to get out of the car and go inside the house.

"Take your shoes off at the door," Mrs. Mulligan said.

I took my time. Instead of just kicking them off like I do at home, I bent down and slowly untied the laces. And while I did that I was listening to see if I could hear the sounds of a dragon moving around downstairs. It was quiet so far but he was probably waiting, maybe even hiding, trying to trick me into thinking it was safe.

"You can go downstairs to play if you like," Mrs. Mulligan said. "There are lots of toys and things down there."

She wasn't fooling me that easily. Let her find some other boy for her dragon to pounce on and poke with its pointy pink tongue!

"Thank you but I don't like to play," I said. "I will just sit here on the couch until my mom or dad gets here."

I thought it was a good idea to remind her that someone was coming for me. She would have a lot of explaining to do if I had disappeared.

"Suit yourself," she said. She plunked down in a chair and I sat on the couch. She picked up a bag with balls of yarn in it and pulled out some knitting needles.

"Do you want to learn to knit?" she asked.

That surprised me. Also, I thought it

could be fun and interesting. I was about to say, "Yes," when I was startled by a lizard running across the floor.

I love lizards and this was the coolest one I've ever seen! Its chin was spiky and fan-shaped, and it looked like it was smiling right at me.

I jumped down off the couch and knelt on the floor. The lizard ran back and forth and all around.

"Can I pick him up?" I asked Mrs. Mulligan.

"Pick who up?" she asked, squinting over her knitting.

"The lizard."

"Oh!" she said. "Yes, go ahead and catch him if you can."

The lizard raced by. I reached out for

him but he was too speedy.

"You'll have to be quick!" Mrs. Mulligan said, shaking her head and laughing. "That scallywag is fast! And he's always getting out of his cage and coming up here."

After a few attempts I got hold of him and held him up to look in his face. He looked grumpy and that made me laugh.

"What's his name?" I asked.

"His name is Dragon," said Mrs. Mulligan. "That kind of lizard is called a bearded dragon, so I thought Dragon would be a fun name for him."

And Dragon smiled and stuck out his pointy pink tongue.